This igloo book belongs to:

....

igloobooks

Published in 2022
First published in the UK by Igloo Books Ltd
An imprint of Igloo Books Ltd
Cottage Farm, NN6 0BJ, UK
Owned by Bonnier Books
Sveavägen 56, Stockholm, Sweden
www.igloobooks.com

1122 006
4 6 8 10 9 7 5
ISBN 978-1-80022-353-0

Written by Stephanie Moss
Illustrated by Kim Barnes

Designed by Jason Shortland
Edited by Daisy Edwards

Printed and manufactured in China

NEVER STOP Believing

igloobooks

I believe that unicorns
aren't just from storybooks.
Until I know it's true, all my
friends can help me look.

I haven't flown to space yet
for a picnic on the moon.
But it's fun to play pretend
when it's a rainy afternoon.

If I meet a mermaid, then I'll ask her for a race.

I'm practising my underwater swimming, just in case.

The heroes in the movies fly like jet planes in the air.
I've met heroes, too. Their powers are to love and care.

I've never seen a fairy, so I think they must be shy.
For now, I'll put my wings on and imagine I can fly.

I believe a monster really is under my bed.

But I'm not afraid. We will be best friends, instead!

I love watching bunnies pop up at a magic show.
I don't ask how they do it, because I don't want to know.

I'd love to join a pirate as they sail the seven seas.

They're welcome on my bathtub ship, but it might be a squeeze.

At bedtime, Mummy always
comes and wishes me sweet dreams.
Then when I close my eyes, I'm sure
I'm dancing on moonbeams.

I believe in things that others might not always see,
and one thing that I'll never stop believing in is...